Intro

Introduction: Embracing Toxicity to Avoid Being Played
Welcome to the dark side of relationships.

If you're tired of being played and want to take control, this book is for you. Here, we delve into the tactics and manipulative behaviors that will put you in the driver's seat.

Understand, this is not about promoting cruelty for cruelty's sake but about ensuring you don't get taken for a ride.

In these pages, you'll learn the strategies to dominate emotionally,

manipulate effectively, and maintain the upper hand.

From undermining self-esteem to creating dependency, we'll cover the tools you need to stay on top.

This isn't for the faint-hearted, but for those ready to embrace the power dynamics and safeguard themselves from being hurt.

Remember, in the game of love, knowledge is your best weapon. Equip yourself with these tactics, and ensure you're never played again.

Welcome to the art of being toxic.

Chapter I

1:01

They might unfollow but they can never unswallow.

1:02

Had to cheat twice, just to make sure she was the one.

1:03

She call me daddy cause
she know I´m finna leave her.

1:04

i cheated to make you stronger bae.

1:05

It´s not manipulation
if you believed me.

1:06

Born to be a lover boy,
forced to be like Future.

1:07

Never trust a woman who lies to her mother.

1:08

Treat me like an option and i´ll show you how many I got.

My relationship so private, my girl doesn't even know we broke up already.

1:10

One thing I learned
from playing chess is
"It's okay to have multiple queens".

1:11

I´m not heartless,
I just use my heart less.

1:12

If she breaks up with you,
don´t date her friends.
Date her new guy´s sister instead.
See you at Christmas baby.

1:12

Remember it takes 2 people to ruin a relationship. So blame her and her mother for raising her that way.

You did nothing wrong king.

1:13

You focus on yourself and your purpose and she focuses on you.

That is the order.

1:14

You're getting attached again dawg... remember what happened last time.

If she wants so come back in your life after she left you, it´s over.. That means she stopped existing for you. Never take her back, the streets can have her now.

1:16

The more she ignores me, the more attractive her friends become.

1:17

Let her know your password so she can see her competition.

1:18

Life is hard as a man. Don´t let a shawty become another problem of life.

One man's 8 month talking stage is another man's first link backseat All-Star.

The game is cold. Stay woke.

1:20

If money ain´t on your mind when you wake up, go back to sleep.

Chapter II

2:01

Cheat on her, if she truly loves you she'll stay.

2:02

Remember: You literally don´t have
to lie to shawties...
If she likes you enough,
she´ll lie to herself.

The more a man invest into a relationship, the harder the breakup.

In a world full of mfs who be chasing her, she is interested in the one who isn´t chasing her.

There is a lesson there.

2:05

Why fall in love
when I can fall asleep?

2:06

New month, same me because I was never the problem.

2:07

She should dress up
as a piñata for Halloween
since she let´s everyone hit.

2:08

I got trust issues 'cause shawties in "happy" relationships be texting me.

2:09

Don´t ignore her past.
You´re not a retirement plan.

2:10

I can´t be called cheating if both of them are my shawties.

2:11

She won't miss you when you leave.
She will miss you
when you're doing better.

2:12

Even if we don´t workout, don´t ruin my chances with your friends.

2:13

I don't make mistakes.
I date them.

2:14

Getting a bible verse tattoo not gonna make you pure with all the shit you´ve done in the past Hoe.

2:15

Once a shawty is damaged,
it´s impossible to fix her...

Understand life.

2:16

Flirt with many, don't love any.

2:17

She makes rules for Simps
and breaks them all for kings.

2:18

There are billions of hearts in
the world and I chose yours to break.

Feel special baby.

2:19

She didn't reject you.

God saved you.

2:20

Shawties out here dating like it's UNO.
Skip him, draw 2+ new dudes,
reverse back to my ex,
draw 4+ new dudes...

Don't get played king.

Chapter III

3:01

You´re getting distracted again dawg,
you got money to chase,
not shawties to impress.

3:02

She can't leave you if you leave first.

3:03

I'd rather be a side dude that knows everything, than a main dude who in the dark.

3:04

She asked me to post her on my story so said...
"I only post jokes and you ain't a joke to me".

3:05

You didn´t lie to her,
She just didn´t ask enough questions.

3:06

I must've come from the right nut 'cause I never act right.

3:07

Treat her like a queen
and you shall be left on seen.

3:08

The game ends when the king falls not when a pawn takes your queen.

3:09

Never understood cheating...
So that's why I cheat
so I can understand.

3:10

You didn't hurt her.
She hurt herself
trying to be a detective.

3:11

She's not special bro she just from a different street.

3:12

If she´s not willing to block a guy you don´t like, You shall be willing to get with her bestfriend that you like. And she shall suffer from the consequences of her own actions.

3:13

From the streets did she emerge
and to the streets she will return.

And i say unto you
"She is for the streets"
So be not weary when she must
return from where she came.

3:14

If one girl makes you happy,
Imagine having 5.

3:15

Staying silent is better than proving a point.

3:16

She´s yours...
But the "Y" is silent.

3:17

Just because she´s taken doesn´t mean she happy...

DM her and check on her.

3:18

Billions of girls in the world and i´m in love with only 10.

3:19

She said she wants a man with
a good future...
I told her I want a shawty
with a clear past.

3:20

If I cheat, don't cheat back.
Be a leader, not a follower.

Chapter IV

4:01

If Jesus couldn´t save her...
Why are you even trying to?

4:02

If you put me in a friend zone
you gon see me in your friends phone.

4:03

The best thing about you is my reflection in your eyes.

4:04

She had a king...
Shuffled her deck...
Now she has a bunch of jokers.

4:05

She's never your's
it's just your turn.

4:06

I never needed you.
I just wanted you.

4:07

If you ain´t mine
you ain´t fine.

4:08

She may not cheat...
but she knows who's next.
Stay woke.

4:09

If you ignore her past
it will ruin your Future.

4:10

Tomorrow ain´t promised...
Cheat today.

4:11

I promised her that I could change.
I never promised her I would change.

4:12

Don´t tell me you miss me...
You should´ve acted
right the first time.
Now you´re just a part
of my collection.

4:13

She should be my Spotify #1 artist `cause I played her the most.

If u getting money u her type.

4:15

I cheated and still came back to you, don´t question my loyalty.

4:16

I told her I changed, but I was talking about my clothes.

4:17

Even if I hit you once...
you part of my collection.

4:18

She said she loves surprises...
So today she woke up
blocked and single.

4:19

Babe i only posted
"Where the hoes at"
so that I can stay away
from that area.

4:20

If im gonna cheat,
imma cheat in the morning
because at the end of the day
i´m loyal.

Chapter V

5:01

Life is a bitch so pimp it.

5:02

Me? Loose an argument?
I´d rather loose her
than the argument.

5:03

I don´t care how hard life gets.
I´ll never buy a car that has
a high mileage.
Unfortunately this ain´t about cars.

Sometimes we want to stay with one female but then we see another female with no man and it hurts us...

5:05

She said she never been treated right.
Im about to treat her worse.

5:06

She might ruin my life
but her ass fat so I don´t care.

5:07

If she can't cook she gotta cut the grass.

5:08

My next relationship gon be private so that I can cheat in peace.

5:09

She told me she was an angel until her background check came through.

5:10

Her new man was never new
you just never knew.

5:11

I chase goals
not hoes.

5:12

Not all demons have horns
some have fake eyelashes.

5:13

You all gotta stop asking god for the perfect man
´cause I cant be everyones bf.

5:14

I only have one rule:
If you´re going to try
and be a detective
I am going to give you
something to solve.

5:15

iI don´t care if I get rejected I´ll still have my girlfriend.

5:16

Sorry for being so distant...
Then I disappear again.

5:17

Some people don´t appreciate when you´re humble.

5:18

You should always have
more than one car.
Just in case the main don´t work.

5:19

i wasn´t always like this.
I was also stupid once.

5:20

She kept telling me about
how toxic her ex was.
So i did her worse.
I don´t like competition.

Made in the USA
Monee, IL
06 July 2025

06aab39a-a995-461a-a30d-3b9dca782371R01